JUST ASK BETTIE ENGLISH

CONNOR WHITELEY

DEDICATION

Thank you to all my readers without you I couldn't do what I love.

PROLOGUE
17th February 2023
7:00 am
Canterbury, England

John Smith had always loved walking in the countryside surrounding Canterbury. The thick large oaks, pines and silver birches were large, imposing and looked like something out of a strange creepy film at night with their huge branches that shot out in all directions.

That was why John really preferred to be out walking in the early hours of the morning. The cold February air was crisp, damp and filled with so much natural goodness that John was so looking forward to his day. His dog Sam would love running up and down the long narrow trail he was walking on now.

The mud moved loudly under his feet, the cold wind howled through the imposing oaks making the branches smash into each other like they were fighting. John really liked it out here and no matter how soul-destroying his office job was, he knew after a day out in the cold forests he would be fine.

Maybe he could talk to Tina today, flirt with her and maybe even ask her out. That would be great.

John kept walking up the long narrow trail, marching through deep dark puddles like they were a child's toy to be stepped over when he noticed something in the distance.

At the very edge of the trail was a boot, a military boot just poking out of the bushes up ahead.

As much as John didn't want to look, he rushed over and he gasped.

In the dark green holly bush at the edge of the trail was a tall man gasping for air, a massive gash across his head made dark rich blood drip down his face into his right eye whilst his left eye focused on John in terror.

John immediately dialled 999 and knelt down on the cold soft mud to get closer to the man. As soon as John was close enough the dying man gripped his t-shirt's collar with a strength John was surprised the man had.

The man gasped and looked like he was trying to speak but no words formed.

The man gasped deeper like he was about to die so John helped lower him to the ground as he knew from his first aid course that the man was going to die. He would die even before an ambulance or paramedics arrived.

The man gestured John to get closer so he did

and he didn't understand what the man's dying words were.

"Just ask Bettie English,"

John just looked at the man as he picked up his phone, checked the time to give the cops an accurate Time of Death and as he started talking to the 999 operator there was a single question that echoed in his mind.

Who the hell was Bettie English?

CHAPTER 1
18:00
17th February 2023
Canterbury, England

Private Eye Bettie English absolutely loved standing in the near-total darkness of her twins' nursery with only a small orange nightlight over each of the white cots for light. The nursery was so peaceful, calm and relaxing that Bettie just loved watching her beautiful, precious children as they drifted off to sleep.

There was nothing more precious in the entire world.

Bettie had really enjoyed making the nursery with her boyfriend Graham the last few months of the pregnancy. They had "debated" which colours to paint the room, what furniture to get and what cot to buy because only the best would do for their precious angels.

Granted Bettie wasn't so sure how much longer

they would be angels, especially with them being six months old now and the fear of them being able to sit up by themselves lurked over her. She loved her kids, but she loved being able to plop them down anywhere and know they would still be there five minutes later, even more.

Bettie always admired the soft blue, red and orange stripes and swirls they had stylishly painted on the walls to give their kids as much visual stimulation as possible. The large lion rug in the middle of the nursery was a great find that Bettie loved sitting on for hours.

There she, Graham or her nephew Sean and his boyfriend read to the kids for hours each night, just spoke to them and basically used them as a soundboard whenever they were stuck on a particular case or Graham just wanted to vent about the nobs at work.

Well, the kids had to hear a lot of words to boost their language development, and sometimes Bettie had her best ideas about investigations after talking to the kids.

The shallow, peaceful sound of their breathing was such a nice little sound over the sheer silence of the house. It was meant to be a peaceful Friday night, Graham was down on the sofa watching some murder programme because clearly they didn't get murder, mayhem and crime in their day jobs and Sean and his boyfriend Harry were out on date night.

Bettie was so looking forward to going

downstairs, spending alone time with the man she loved and not having a single crime to solve in the meantime.

The day had been chaotic with the twins doing a lot of "talking" to each other, wanting to constantly smash down all the block towers her and Graham made for them and the twins seemed to be the most energetic today than they ever had been before.

Bettie was refusing to take that as a scary sign of her future as a mother. But after three conference calls with different companies, her staff at the British Private Eye Federation and a catering company for an event coming up in the Private Eye calendar, Bettie was so looking forward to a nice relaxing evening with her boyfriend.

All whilst her little angels slept peacefully.

"Bet," Graham said so quietly she wasn't sure she had actually heard anything.

Bettie looked around at Graham who was still beautiful even in the darkness of the bedroom door.

"Need you downstairs soon," Graham said.

Bettie nodded. She had no idea why but she loved him and she trusted him, maybe he was planning something romantic. Bettie just grinned and blew Graham a kiss as he nodded and walked away.

She went over to the little white cot tucked lovingly away in opposite corners of the nursey and so badly wanted to kiss her little darlings on the cheek before she went downstairs, but she didn't dare wake them.

They looked so small, cute and precious as their tiny chests rose and fell peacefully, Harrison and Elizabeth had to be the cutest kids she had ever seen. Bettie supposed she had to say that but it was the truth.

Bettie waved her little darlings goodnight and she went out the nursery, down their long hallway to their brown staircase and went down it.

Maybe she should have freshened up a little because Graham was clearly going to be romantic for a change, she probably should have put her perfume on and maybe she should have changed her underwear to the little lacy pair that Graham got her on Valentine's day.

But they were basically married in all but name, they both had careers and two even more amazing kids. They didn't always need to go all out in the romance department (going all out was what made them have kids in the first place) but as Bettie went down into the kitchen she just frowned.

Graham wasn't being romantic in the slightest because there was a man in a black three-piece suit sitting at their large marble kitchen island in their large copper-finished kitchen with a police badge sitting on its freshly polished surface and Graham was sitting opposite him like they were best friends.

Bettie felt so under dressed in her black jogging bottoms, hoody and socks. All her conference calls had been online so there was no point changing into something nice and it was too cold to go out so she hadn't dressed up at all.

Graham was still in jeans, a posh hoody and black shoes so compared to the cop he looked amazing or average.

Bettie just folded her arms and looked at the man she loved.

"Bettie, this is Detective Kinsley, homicide division and he has some questions to ask you because a dead man said you knew what happened to him," Graham said.

Bettie just grinned. Her quiet evening was as dead as the man they were talking about but Bettie had to admit this excited her a lot more than she ever had the right to feel.

CHAPTER 2
18:15

17th February 2023

Canterbury, England

Graham just watched as the sexy woman he loved climbed up onto the red plastic bar stools that they had circling the great marble kitchen island that Graham had to fight for so long to get, Bettie was so damn beautiful and the entire copper kitchen just seemed to accent her stunning beauty.

Graham had never ever been sure before on a copper kitchen but it was the best decision him and Bettie had ever made. All the cabinets and cupboards were finished with a copper coating that made the light shine and dazzle and memorise in a stunning way and with white marble worktops the copper worked even better if such a thing was possible.

Graham looked at Detective Kinsley who had just sat back down again after making Bettie a fresh mug of coffee (the only thing she had got back too after her pregnancy). He knew the Detective from work and he was a great officer, very passionate, very good and very rule focused. He didn't actually think Detective Kinsley could break a rule even if his life depended on it.

His suit looked good and considering that Kinsley was still very young for a detective, Graham was sort of glad that Sean and Harry were on date night. The last thing he wanted was the nephew he loved like his own twins, staring at Kinsley constantly.

Graham could perfectly understand it. Kinsley was fit, clean shaven and his suit definitely suggested that there were massive biceps, six-pack and a fit body underneath them but still.

"What's this about then?" Bettie asked.

Graham was really put off by the sheer silence of the house and Kinsley. The TV was off, the babies were thankfully sound asleep and everything was silent so this had to be important. Graham seriously didn't want to be involved in another murder just yet.

The sweet aromas of coffee, ice cream and salted caramel (vegan of course) filled the air from their dessert and Graham loved the sweet taste of the ice cream that formed on his tongue. And he actually wished he had some of it with him now, he felt like he was going to need it.

"At 7 o'clock this morning a walker found the body of a dying man and his dying words were *just ask Bettie English,*" Detective Kinsley said.

Graham just looked at Bettie. He was fairly sure

his girlfriend hadn't killed or attacked anyone.

"I don't know who you're talking about. I'm not aware of any plot, threats or attacks against me, my people or anyone else," Bettie said wrapping her hands around her mug.

Graham was so relieved to hear that. As much as he loved Bettie being the President of the British Private Eye Federation he did hate the amount of death threats she got. Thankfully, they were just nutters that wanted to spread hate.

Kinsley nodded. "Then I'm sorry to tell you that victim was called Frank Lee. Do you know him?"

Graham had no idea who the man was so he just looked at Bettie.

Bettie nodded. "He was an old, old school friend of mine. We weren't best friends or anything but from years 7 to the end of sixth form we were always sitting next to each other in class. He was a great guy. What happened?"

Kinsley looked at Graham so he gestured the Detective to continue.

Kinsley passed them both crime scene photos and Graham was surprised. It was definitely an isolated trail surrounding Canterbury, the wound was deep across his face clearly made by a knife or something sharp and he had been pushed into the bushes. Someone didn't want him found.

"Why didn't they hide the body better or make sure he was dead?" Bettie asked.

"We aren't sure but I expect the walker

interrupted the killer," Kinsley said.

Graham folded his arms. "It's been almost 12 hours since you found the body I take it. Why has it taken you all day to come and see Bettie?"

Kinsley smiled. "I know she's the President of the Federation. If she was involved then I needed to make sure I had proof. Solid proof,"

Graham nodded that was a good idea. At least Kinsley wasn't stupid.

Graham looked down for his mug of drink but he never made himself one, something he would have to fix in a moment.

"So what have you found?" Bettie asked.

Kinsley bit his lip. "What exactly was your friend involved in?"

Bettie shrugged. "I don't know. We tried to keep in contact during university but he stopped returning my calls and texts. I haven't thought about the man for years,"

"The victim had to be involved in some sort of criminal activity because when we searched his home we discovered this single email waiting for us,"

Graham didn't like the sound of that at all. Who the hell left the police a message after they were killed or the killer left the message.

Kinsley showed them his phone and Graham gasped at the message. It read *Just Ask Bettie English before the attack tomorrow at 6 am.*

Graham just shook his head. It was clear that they wanted the police or someone to suspect Bettie, but what the hell did Bettie have to do with all of this?

"What attack?" Bettie asked. "And just for your information I know nothing about this,"

Kinsley nodded. "That is our working theory too. As soon as you left school we cannot find any connection or contact between you two. We also have no idea what the attack could be,"

Graham rolled his eyes. That was great.

Graham was just about to pop off his bar stool to make himself a cup of coffee when the lights went off.

That was a little weird but as Graham turned around to see where Bettie was and if she was okay he realised that he couldn't see the street lights, high street lights or the cathedral lights in Canterbury.

The entire area had fallen into darkness.

They were in a blackout with a murder to solve, two sleeping babies who hated the dark upstairs and a killer planning an attack of some sort.

A blackout certainly wasn't going to help.

CHAPTER 3
18:45
17th February 2023
Canterbury, England

"Just drive home safely okay. Actually no forget the car just walk back. Traffic lights won't be working. Love you,"

As soon as the lights went out Bettie knew she had to protect her children, who Sean and Harry basically were at this point, so she called them and made them promise her to stay safe.

As Bettie, Graham and Kinsley all stood or sat around the kitchen table in complete and utter darkness as the reality of the situation sank in, Bettie just couldn't believe what the hell was happening. Frank was a great man, kind man and one of her best friends at school even though she never liked to admit it because he was part of the wargaming nerd group of school.

Oh God, Bettie hated that she used to think like

that, but she was young, stupid and she was part of the popular crowd. She always made sure Frank was okay and enjoying school but, ah why didn't she just allow him to sit with them at lunch. Why didn't she stand up for him more?

Bettie forced herself to take a long deep breath of the coffee-scented air and she focused on what she could do for Frank now. The poor man was dead, she had to get justice.

But she had no idea why Frank wanted everyone to talk to her like she would know exactly what was going on. Maybe she did, her and Frank had had some great conversations in third-period biology over the years, it was great fun and some of the discussions were weird.

Maybe those conversations were the key to everything. They were over twenty years ago, but Bettie had to focus on them later on.

"I think we have a backup generator in the back," Graham said.

Bettie smiled through the darkness. Of all the bloody toys that Graham had bought and she wanted to prove to him a generator was a silly idea this was the very last thing she needed. Making Graham think he was wise seemed to be a very dangerous idea to give him.

She did love him.

"I'll go and set up the generator. I think I left it out in the sun for enough months last year for it to be charged," Graham said.

Bettie waved her hands about but then realise they were in pitch darkness so no one could see her.

"Wait. Let's come up with a game plan first of all before we go off, and you need a torch anyway," Bettie said.

"Oh yeah," Graham said.

"Detective Kinsley I take it you want our help solving this murder right?"

"Yes please and I'll have to call National Power but I doubt an attack on the power grid was the 6 am target,"

Bettie had to agree. She knew that Frank had been fascinated with the power grid and they had debated all lesson once about what an attack on the power grid would mean for society. Then Frank had always a good plan in theory and everything.

He was rubbish and next to useless doing anything practical. It was why he failed Engineering, cooking and PE.

"Why me?" Bettie asked herself.

"Maybe call your friends at the Federation?" Kinsley asked. "The computers at Kent Police would be shut down,"

"I'll do that in a minute," Bettie said.

She had debated for months about moving the headquarters of the Federation from London to Canterbury just so it was easier for her but now she was never going to do that.

"What else have you found out today?" Bettie asked.

"Not a lot. We searched his home, found some samples of something, took his computers and his lab equipment. Zoey is still testing those. I don't know if she has any results just yet,"

Bettie nodded. They had to contact Zoey in a minute then as well.

"What about his work?" Graham asked.

"I know Frank worked for a computer company in Canterbury called Protectus. A low-level security firm that deals with commercial property nothing connected to a power grid bear in mind. Everyone loved him,"

Bettie just shook her head in the darkness. If she wasn't so concerned about making sure she had enough phone battery and charge on her laptop she would do some research on the company but she didn't.

An immense boom echoed all around Canterbury.

Huge sparks and explosions lit up the sky in three places in the distance.

Bettie swore under her breath. She really hoped the sound didn't wake the babies but she also knew exactly what the explosions were.

The phone towers in and surrounding Canterbury were now destroyed.

Bettie took out her phone and just shook her head as she saw she had no service. No way to call the Federation, no way to call for support or help in any fashion whatsoever.

Even if the power was restored quickly they still couldn't call anyone for days or maybe even weeks.

And with the power gone the Wi-Fi was down and with the phone towers destroyed Mobile Data was also out of the question.

Someone was clearly going to a lot of effort to make sure no one could or would contact anyone in Canterbury.

Bettie was completely alone and now she had no idea whatsoever how to solve this crime.

Not a clue at all.

CHAPTER 4
19:15
17 February 2023
Canterbury, England

Graham seriously wasn't interested as he stumbled back into the kitchen using the bright white light from his torch after reading the instructions of the solar power generator in the shelter. Whilst it could power the entire house and all their devices, now that the phone towers were destroyed, there was still no service.

And Graham had never bought the adapter needed to actually connect it to the house and as Bettie leant on the kitchen island, Graham really wanted to kiss that smiling face that mocked him silently.

"At least we can charge our devices when we need to," Bettie said. "But I would prefer some main lights too,"

Graham just stuck his tongue out at her, and he

had to admit that he was really glad that the babies were still peacefully sleeping upstairs. He hated to even imagine how hard it would be to calm them down if they woke up with their night lights not working.

"I think we have to split up now," Bettie said, "with one of us staying in the house to make sure the babies are okay,"

Kinsley sounded like he was about to say something when his walkie-talkie sounded and Graham recognised it as one of the new, smaller devices that Kent Police were trialling out.

Kinsley put it up to his ear and Graham hoped it wasn't more bad news. He felt like they needed Kinsley to help solve this but this was the police's worse nightmare. All the criminals and thieves and robbers would be out on the street tonight taking full advantage of the blackout.

Graham was just glad that their security did run off a solar-powered generator built into the system so hopefully everything would still be okay.

"Of course sir," Kinsley said as he turned to Graham. "I'm sorry but they're extending my shift and I have to go and patrol the high street. Can you solve it without me?"

Graham just looked at the woman he loved through the torchlight and just grinned.

"I think we can manage," Bettie said.

Kinsley smiled. "Good. Graham, we're operating on Channel 16 if you need anything,"

Graham just nodded and he had completely forgotten that he had been "gifted" a police radio last week. It was hiding away in a closest but he was definitely going to get that.

"We're home," Sean said from the living room.

"In here," Bettie said.

Graham just grinned as even through the pitch darkness of the living room he could still see Sean's stylish pink highlights in his longish blond hair with another dark figure behind him.

Bettie focused her torchlight on Kinsley and Graham forced himself not to laugh so he focused his torchlight on Sean and Harry as they walked in wearing their white shirts, black shoes and black trousers. They clearly went somewhere very fancy for date night.

"It's chaos out there. Traffic awful. Cars are crashing and- holy fuck," Sean said.

Graham just laughed as Sean's mouth dropped and Harry walked into the back of him and he also smiled a little.

Then Harry hit his boyfriend. "Not that hot,"

Graham smiled. Whilst Harry's recovery from his brain injury last June was still a slow work in progress like it was for everyone after the first six months, it was still great to see that he had a great personality.

Kinsley looked a little flushed and Graham had no idea he was gay before now.

"Um I better, yeah, I better go," Kinsley said.

Graham hugged Bettie as they both laughed so

hard that no sound came out. They loved Sean and Harry, they were amazing young men.

"You two can stop pissing yourself now," Sean said.

Graham kissed Bettie and forced himself to breathe. "Sorry we just wanted to see if you found him hot,"

Sean smiled but just hugged Harry. "Yeah he's hot but I only love Harry," he said giving his boyfriend a massive kiss on the cheek that made Harry blush so bright he might as well have been a nightlight.

"What happen?" Harry asked.

Graham spent the next few minutes telling Sean and Harry everything they knew so far and what had happened to Frank.

Sean nodded as he took a torch out of a kitchen draw. "I think we have to admit this blackout is weird and the destruction of the phone towers too,"

Graham nodded. If it was just the blackout he wouldn't think it was weird at all but the phone towers just tipped it over the edge.

"You two do Advanced Technological Engineering," Bettie said. "Any help or insight?"

Harry huffed like this was a massive ask. "Was module on grid week last,"

"True," Sean said. "Basically, the power grid is a massive computer and mechanical system. Computers control where the power goes and flows to. It isn't easy to hack or even control. It's ambitious so I think they attacked the substation that serves Canterbury."

Graham shrugged at Bettie. All he knew about the national grid was that it was what allowed him to charge his phone at night and have a nice hot shower with Bettie in the morning.

"Besides from that we would have to read our textbooks and of course, textbooks don't include the ins and outs of how to attack a substation,"

Bettie grinned and Graham pulled her closer. That was a good point. Of course, in normal times they would just look it up online or call a friend that would know.

They couldn't do that today.

"I want to see Zoey and see if she remembers the test results," Bettie said. "Someone has to stay here to watch the kids,"

"We'll watch the kids and try to learn more about the attack. At least that would give us an idea of the power of the people behind it,"

Graham nodded that was perfect. "And I'll go to the address of Protectus. I know the address and maybe they're still there because of the blackout. Trying to secure data files or whatever tech companies do?"

Harry laughed and Graham knew he had no idea what tech companies did, but at least everyone had a plan and hopefully they would learn something.

Hopefully before it was all too late.

CHAPTER 5
19:45
17th February 2023
Canterbury, England

As Bettie finally finished the long walk to her best friend Forensic Specialist Zoey Quill's house she was really starting to miss the modern world. She had already seen three car crashes and three groups of very dodgy people walking about.

Thankfully, Graham had insisted that she went out with a kitchen knife and taser in her black purse and she was really glad she had listened. It was chaos out on the streets tonight.

She just hoped that Graham would be okay too, and if anyone could keep the house safe it was definitely Sean and Harry. They had done it before so they could easily do it again.

Bettie stood on Zoey's large white front door that almost glowed in the pitch darkness of the long street with semi-detached houses lining it. She had been here plenty of times before but in the darkness it looked creepy.

All the houses looked identical like she was in some strange and creepy American subdivision and wanted to kill all the fun and uniqueness of each property. Bettie was glad her house didn't look like that but at least Zoey's house was the one look with a brilliant rose garden out front with bright vivid shades of reds, yellows and whites shining in the darkness.

Bettie knocked on the door as the sweet scents of the roses filled her senses and made the taste of spring picnics with her mother and sister form on her tongue.

Then she realised that Zoey might not be answering the door in case she was a robber or someone.

"Open up Zoey. It's Bettie. It's about a case," she shouted as she banged on the door.

A few moments later, Zoey opened the door gesturing her inside and it was only when Bettie shone her torch at Zoey's tracksuit that she realised Zoey was holding the heaviest frying pan she had.

"Thanks for not knocking me out," Bettie said focusing on Zoey shutting, locking and bolting the front door shut.

A lot of people might have seen that as overkill but it seriously wasn't. They all worked with dead people for a living so they knew exactly what a human could do to another if they really wanted to.

"How are your kids?" Zoey asked taking Bettie by the hand and leading her somewhere. It was so dark in the house Bettie was grateful for it.

"Good thanks. They're sleeping through it all. How about yours?"

"Husband upstairs now sleeping with the kids. They didn't want to go to bed without one of us. I'm too stressed to go to bed and I don't want to make kids feel my stress too," Zoey said.

Bettie just nodded. She always knew that Zoey was a good mum and always wanted the best for her kids but this was just so hard on both of them.

Bettie allowed herself to be led into a large living room that was covered in hundreds of little tealights that Bettie imagined would be rather romantic if they weren't in the middle of a blackout.

Zoey carefully made space on a small black sofa for Bettie to sit down on and Bettie smiled at her best friend as Zoey started shaking.

Bettie hugged her and gently stroked her back like her mother had done when she was a teenager scared of something, a boy, an event or something happening in the world.

"What if someone attacks me and my family? I've sent a lot of criminals away," Zoey said.

Bettie wanted to agree but that so wasn't a good idea at the moment. Normally she would call someone from the Federation's protection unit to come and protect Zoey but she couldn't.

"I'll protect you but I need to know did you

finish running the tests on Frank. Any biological samples collected, anything on the body, anything else from the house?" Bettie asked.

Zoey sat up perfectly straight. "I submitted everything to the detective just before I left at 5 but I guess everyone's been too busy to read it,"

Bettie supposed that was true and it wasn't like anyone could look at their emails now.

"I remember I didn't find anything interesting in the samples from the body and the head wound contained traces of medical-grade metal. The same stuff that scalpels are made from,"

Bettie hated dealing with rogue medical professionals but she really doubted a group of doctors could destroy the power grid.

"It seemed that your friend Frank was collecting hair samples from different people. They showed signs of DNA extraction and that was what all his lab equipment seemed to be about. It was a beautiful lab by the way,"

Bettie flat out had no idea why a man working at a computer company was so interested in DNA extraction. Hell she had no idea how it worked.

"What about his computer?" Bettie asked.

Zoey laughed. "Forensically cleaned before the police got to the house. There was a programme that activated at 7 am this morning that wiped everything and made sure the message the police found was seen on the screen,"

That was weird.

"Is it possible Frank did all this? Or did someone else do it?"

Zoey shrugged. "No way to know for sure obviously but I looked at the code and everything and it's possible the programme was secretly installed when Frank downloaded an email attachment once. I don't know who it's from though,"

Bettie nodded. That was a sign at least and something she could use.

Something tapped against the wall. Zoey slowly picked up her frying pan as Bettie saw something move in the darkness and it sounded like something was scratching against the front door wanting to get in.

"I told you someone's after me," Zoey said.

Bettie stood up and slowly went over to the entrance to the living room.

A little girl ran out towards Zoey.

"Mummy!" the girl shouted.

Zoey quickly put down the frying pan and scooped up her daughter in her arms.

"Daddy snores. I can't sleep,"

Bettie just laughed and before she decided on what to do next she just wanted to make sure Zoey would be okay alone. She must have received some death threats lately or something because she was never this jumpy before.

Bettie just had to make sure that her best friend was okay but the threat was real. She knew someone could be after all of them by the time this was over.

CHAPTER 6
20:15
17th February 2023
Canterbury, England

Scared little women always ran away like little stupid mice whenever there was danger. That was a simple fact that Toby Stevens knew all too well.

He simply stood behind a large bush of some little plant across the street from where the evil Zoey Quill lived and he watched intensely as his pray rushed off with Bettie English with a large frying pan.

Toby was dressed in all black and he was patient, calm, collective. He normally used those skills to help train young boys and girls on his local football team, he used those skills to show young people how to cook at the local homeless kitchen and he even used his patient skills to help teach refugees English.

He loved all of those innocent people because they were the future of the world and he truly loved them.

But as he watched the evil Zoey Quill walk away from her house with Bettie, he was determined to end her miserable life and make sure he never got attacked with that damn frying pan.

Toby had to admit the frying pan was a cute, pathetic touch but it wouldn't save her.

Zoey Quill was a cold, evil woman that made a living off destroying lives with her science and her tests. She sent people away from their families, away from their lives and she basically gave people a death sentence.

Toby hated Zoey Quill with all his heart. If only Zoey hadn't been so good at her evil job then maybe his father would still be alive. His father had never meant to kill his mother but she was foul, abusive and always beating him.

But yeah he was the evil one.

It had been so quick that murder. That simple act had opened Toby's eyes to the possibilities of life outside the law but Zoey Quill had put his father behind bars.

The simple act that made his father get stabbed in the prison washing rooms only two weeks after he had been sent there by the most evil woman on the planet.

So now she had to pay. She had to suffer. She had to die.

CHAPTER 7
20:15
17th February 2023

Canterbury, England

Graham seriously had to admit that it was a flat out stupid idea to drive anywhere in Canterbury tonight. Thankfully the traffic was better because no one was stupid enough to try and drive in a blackout, groups of people had still thrown beer bottles at Graham's car and some idiots were driving without their lights on.

The dicks.

Finally, Graham arrived at the headquarters of Protectus just outside Canterbury. It was a beautiful large glass building that went up two stories and allowed Graham to see everything inside because a backup generator must have kicked in.

The bright orange lights inside shone like beacons of hope in the foul darkness that had covered Canterbury, Graham's eyes almost ached from just seeing the light. His eyes were used to the darkness now so the bright light was a little too intense.

The icy cold air wrapped around Graham making him shiver as he peeked into the headquarters hoping to see some movement or a sign that a person was inside and hopefully that person could help him find out what happened to Frank.

The air smelt damp, cold and hints of pine littered too reminding Graham of adventures he had had as a child with his dad before he died. But now all that he wanted was to see a sign that someone was inside.

A moment later a very tall woman in a leopard-spotted dress and ten-inch heels walked out into view.

Graham banged on the window showing her his police ID.

The woman walked straight up to the window and smiled at Graham, he actually had to look up to see her face.

The woman focused on his police badge like he was a fake and she looked like she was about to ask him to leave.

"I am real and I'm investigating a murder," Graham said.

"What happened to Kinsley?" the woman shouted through the glass.

Graham gestured that he wanted to come up and after a few moments the woman rolled her eyes and ushered Graham inside through a large reinforced glass door a few metres to Graham's left.

The inside was so nice and warm that Graham shivered in pleasure, the large circular lobby of the headquarters was so peaceful and modern with chairs and desks made of sterile white plastic that made the entire place look stunning.

The woman folded her arms and frowned. "I am Gloria Chatham, the owner of Protectus. I am busy making sure everything is protected from the power surge that will happen when the grid is bought back online. Can we please keep this short?"

Graham nodded and Gloria gestured him to walk with her so he nodded.

Gloria led Graham towards a small black fire door that presumably lead to something computer related.

"Do you know anyone who would want Frank harmed?"

Gloria shook her head. "I've already told Kinsley everything,"

"He's been reassigned because of the blackout and as it's my day off he wanted me to investigate it,"

"You and Bettie English you mean,"

Graham nodded. He was always surprised that everyone knew who he was because of Bettie.

"He, Frank I mean, was always talking about Bettie. Whenever she was in the paper he was so proud of her, when she got voted in as the President he was the proudest person alive and he actually recommended her to us. She helped us a few years ago. Great, great woman,"

Graham was impressed. But why was Frank so interested in Bettie if they hadn't spoken for twenty years?

"Did he ever say why he didn't call her or text her back?"

Gloria stopped dead in her tracks and looked around like there might be someone listening in.

Graham went close to her. "What's going on?"

"Frank was not normal in some regards you know. He once told me he had taken the job promotion I had given him not to better himself. But so all the extra money could go towards Project Blackout,"

Graham's stomach tightened. "What was this project?"

"I don't know he was pretty drunk when he told me and the others but I think he was looking for the perfect way to attack the power grid,"

Graham couldn't understand it. It wasn't a normal thing to do.

"Why?" Graham asked.

"I have no idea. Everything here is working, there is no evil code in the backup systems. I would have expected that to happen. There is nothing work-related that I can think of," Gloria said.

"What about outside of work?"

Gloria went over to the small black fire door and rolled her head side to side like she had a kink in her neck.

"I don't know if it's relevant but at his first Christmas party when he came here. He was talking to Gill, great middle-aged woman who died of cancer three months ago. You see she lost her children because of disease on his 20th birthday, apparently Frank was talking to her about finding lost children,"

Graham just cocked his head. Why in the world would Frank want to find a lost child? By all records he didn't have a girlfriend, wife or any legal sign that he had a child. All Kinsley had found for a next of Kin was a brother in Wales.

He didn't have a social life outside of work from what Kinsley could find so why was Frank interested in a child?

"I'm sorry detective but that's all I can say. I don't know anything else and I have work to do," Gloria said.

Graham started walking away when he asked, "Where did Frank work before this job?"

Gloria shrugged. "I actually have no idea. All I know is that he appeared with a very official glowing recommendation from a company that didn't exist. I'm a former White Hat hacker, I think we both know what that means,"

Graham just nodded and thanked her time. If Gloria used to hack for the UK government and defend its cyber infrastructure then he knew that Frank probably did something for the Government as well.

But what? And finding out in the middle of a

blackout was going to be next to impossible.

CHAPTER 8
20:30
17th February 2023
Canterbury, England

After comforting Zoey for a while, listening to how she had received ten death threats from the exact same man in the past week and how she was starting to fear for her life, Bettie was absolutely steaming and she actually suggested that Zoey come with her. Especially as all the letters said how the man wouldn't attack her husband or children.

The man only wanted to kill her, and her alone.

As Zoey's small black Ford pulled into the gravel driveway of Frank's small bungalow a mile away from the high street, Bettie had to admit that Frank's house looked great.

Its small yellow bricks added a certain charm to the place, the little sweetpea garden with a few peas and tomato plants made the air smell delightful and it was even better that the large blue front door was sealed up tight so no one could go in.

Bettie heard footsteps coming from the back and before she could go into the back garden, a very short little man walked up wearing a cop uniform. He had a massive flashlight and a walkie talkie so presumably he was real.

Bettie shone her torch low in his direction and he did the same, she knew that Zoey was firmly behind her raising her frying pan that she had insisted on bringing along.

"Who are you?" the cop asked.

"Bettie English, Private Eye, and this is Zoey Quill,"

The man nodded like he wanted to let them in but it knew ultimately destroyed the integrity of the crime scene.

"We took over the case from Detective Kinsley. We want to look around the house and to see what you guys missed," Bettie said.

"I do not miss anything," the cop said.

Bettie rolled her eyes in the pitch darkness, there was going to be an attack in less than nine hours and this man was more focused on his ego. Typical, just typical.

More footsteps banging against the pavement outside made Bettie look around and it was a group of young women who were laughing, shouting and were clearly as high as a kite.

As much as Bettie knew there was a tiny chance of them being attacked, she still didn't want to be on the streets if possible for any longer than needed.

A car pulled up next outside and Bettie smiled as Graham stood up out of the car and smiled.

The cop immediately saluted Graham like he was a war hero.

"It's okay Jim. I'll look after the civilian help on this case. You just look outside and guard the perimeter, okay?" Graham asked.

Bettie wasn't sure she liked being called Civilian help but she wasn't going to argue if it got them access to the crime scene.

Graham gestured them over to the front door, he cut the seal and the three of them went inside.

It was clear as day to Bettie that the entire place was a messy death trap with mouldy takeaway containers, rubbish littering the hallway's floor and there was another smell that Bettie didn't even want to identify.

The three of them went into the so-called living room were the body was found, and it wasn't really a living room by any definition. There were two large blue sofas and a TV mounted onto the wall but that was were the typical living room stuff ended.

There was a huge blackwood desk tucked away in one corner where the body was found, Bettie and the others put on their gloves and they went over to it. Bettie didn't really want to look at the two dining tables full of DNA extraction equipment for now, and that was definitely more of Zoey's domain anyway.

Bettie carefully picked through the blood covered letters, pens and notepads after Graham confirmed to them that everything was okay to touch because it had been photographed at least three times.

The first notepads Bettie picked up was a list of private eyes that she knew really well. Some of them were her best friends and her name was repeated constantly with private phone numbers next to each name.

Some of them appeared to be crossed out but in no particular order, Bettie couldn't understand why next to her name was written *Don't Call Until They Betray You*.

That was flat out weird. If Frank knew that he was going to be betrayed or there was a chance of betrayal then why didn't he get help sooner? Why was he even looking up private eyes?

Bettie shook her head. This was making no sense so she opened up the second notepad on the desk and it was filled with names of people and there was a column next to it saying whether their hair had been collected yet or not.

There weren't that many more people to get hair samples from but it was still strange, and a single question kept coming back to Bettie. Why was a man that worked in a computer place so interested in hair samples?

Then Bettie picked up the last notepad that was labelled *The Case of The Lost Child*.

"That's what his boss said he was interested in,"

Graham said.

Bettie nodded as she opened it. There was only a single page written out in the notepad and only made things weirder.

"He wrote," Bettie said, "about a child that went missing at birth. Oh this was his brother, his brother was meant to have died at birth but because the parents donated the body to medical science. The hospital it was donated to rejected the body because they believed the parents had stolen the baby themselves. The DNA wasn't a match to theirs,"

"God, just imagining going through the torture of losing a kid only to find out it wasn't yours anyway?" Graham said.

Bettie could only nod at that. "Then Frank wrote about how he had Haemophilia A and he wrote in a local newspaper article about someone who looked like him. He thought that was his brother,"

Zoey nodded and shone her torch at Bettie a little more. "That condition is genetic so that explains the DNA extraction. Hair contains DNA so Frank was extracting the DNA of these people to see if he could find his brother,"

Bettie wanted to agree and she did for the most part but nothing made any sense.

"If this is true," Bettie said, "how does this relate to the power grid being knocked out, mobile service being knocked out and an attack in less than 9 hours?"

Zoey and Graham frowned and Bettie agreed

there. None of them had any clue how these strange pieces fitted together.

Not a damn clue.

CHAPTER 9
22:00
17th February 2023
Canterbury, England

After spending two long hours searching the house, finding and double-checking Frank's DNA results and watching sexy Bettie fall asleep for ten minutes, Graham was partly annoyed they hadn't found anything of interest but he was even more happy to be home.

Sean and Harry had placed little tealights, large candles and torches all over the living room and as the five of them all sat on Graham's two large black sofas, Graham pulled Bettie close to him. The living room felt so romantic with all the candles and if he was so damn tired he would have been kissing, hugging and seducing Bettie like no tomorrow.

Graham fought to keep his eyelids open but he just focused on Sean, Harry and Zoey who sat on the other sofa. Everyone had large mugs of strong battery-acid strength coffee. Thank God they had a gas cooker so they could still boil the water.

Graham was never ever getting rid of that gas cooker now. It was a lifeline and if the power cut continued into tomorrow then he was just glad he could still cook the kids' dinner and everything.

Sean took a sip of his coffee. "Me and Harry read a lot of the literature on substations and it's complex but to put it simply. It is perfectly possible that if someone attacked a substation then it could knock out power to an area,"

Graham nodded, at least their theory was correct.

"Mainly because," Sean said, "it is a substation had takes the power from 450 volts down to a safe level that won't make the house explode when it receives the power. Without a substation, no power can get to the houses,"

Graham was surprised when Bettie pushed herself into his warmth. He liked that a lot.

"What about the computer theory?" Zoey asked.

Sean and Harry just looked at each other. Harry looked like he wanted to say something but he was getting annoyed at himself. Sean just kissed him and turned to everyone.

"That's the problem. There are no real computer systems to hack into at a substation. To disable a substation you need to either pull the breaker and stop someone from lifting it back up,"

"Like we do to reset the fuses in our house," Bettie said.

Sean nodded. "Exactly. Or you need to cause an explosion and the textbook example if throwing a shopping trolley into a substation so the electricity goes it and it explodes and causes all types of problems,"

Graham kissed Bettie on the head. That meant that their criminals weren't just computer experts and-

Graham shook his hands in the air. "Wait, why are we working on the theory that these criminals are computer experts?"

Bettie sat up. "Damn it you're right. We only worked on the assumption because we fought the national grid was hacked or something,"

"But if our textbooks are right," Sean said, "which for the price of them I hope they are. Then hackers make no sense here,"

Zoey nodded. "You probably only thought about the hackers because Frank worked as a computer person at Protectus,"

"True," Graham said. "But remember I mentioned about Frank working for the government. I doubt he was a computer expert for the government, so what was he?"

"He not work for big company," Harry said.

Graham completely agreed. All the former government, MI5 and GCHQ employees always went to work for massive computer companies. They certainly don't work for a small company like Protectus.

Graham took a large sip of his strong wonderfully bitter coffee, and he was still so glad that the kids seemed to be sleeping through the night so far. He only wished he was that lucky.

Bettie stood up and paced for a moment. "What if Frank was a biological expert or something? I know biology was his favourite science as a kid. What if he went to university to study biology?"

"Makes sense but what uni did he go to?" Graham asked.

"University of Bath. We can't call them because of the time, let alone the fact we don't have power," Bettie said.

Graham sighed. He just wanted a single break in the case but that seemed to be flat out impossible.

"Are we stuck?" Sean asked grinning.

Graham threw his arms up in the air. "We know that Frank was murdered by a slice-"

Zoey jumped up in excitement. "Remember he was a haemophiliac. Even a small cut or slice in the right position could have killed him,"

Bettie and Graham nodded. Graham looked at the beautiful woman he loved. "You think this wasn't murder?"

Bettie shook her head. "Maybe but he was still attacked with a scalpel or something and, damn it. I think we need an hour's rest,"

The entire room went silent and as much as Graham wanted to argue, stress that there was an attack coming and they couldn't waste time and they needed to solve this immediately. He knew she was right.

"I agree," Graham said. "Me and Bettie will sit down here so we can watch the candles. Make sure the house doesn't burn down. Sean and Harry go to bed until 11 and Zoey take our bed,"

Zoey didn't seem sure.

"I changed the bedding earlier," Bettie said smiling.

Zoey nodded and the three of them went upstairs. Graham kissed Bettie's neck.

"You know you changed the bedding early Monday morning. It's Friday,"

Bettie quietly laughed and shrugged. "She needs sleep and I want her to feel safe. A little lie won't hurt her,"

Graham just smiled and shook his head. He so badly wanted a nap and then hopefully they could solve this impossible case.

CHAPTER 10
23:30
17th February 2023

Canterbury, England

Damn stupid alarm.

Bettie really hated her stupid alarm app on her phone. It was meant to wake them up by 11 pm but it had woken them up 30 minutes later. That was just flat out annoying.

As Bettie sat up perfectly straight on the black sofa next to the sleeping love of her life with the refreshing hints of strong black coffee welcoming her into the land of the awoken, she actually had an idea about the case and she felt amazing.

It had been ages since she had struggled on a case like this, had to work such long hours and been filled with such a massive amount of fear. But Bettie truly believed that every single thing did come back to the missing brother.

Bettie carefully stood up making sure that

Graham's head was supported as she allowed him to sleep a little longer, and she went into the kitchen where she had put a bunch of evidence bags they had bought back from Frank's house.

She put on gloves and flicked through the hair sample notepad containing all the names he wanted to collect samples from. The weird thing about the pad was that it collected a lot of female names with a small downwards arrows.

And after a few minutes of flicking through the female names, Bettie realised that these were children.

Bettie had to admit that was clever. Clearly there had to be some people that Frank couldn't get to so instead of collecting DNA samples from the father, he went to the children or at least wanted to, because none of the children's names had ticks next to them.

Bettie climbed up onto a barstool and just couldn't believe what was happening.

She honestly felt like such a dick for how she had treated her best friend at secondary school. Sure he had been a science-obsessed nerd, she had been a popular girl with all the friends, status and power.

Bettie had only allowed poor Frank to spend time with her whenever they shared a class, they texted at times and they called each other maybe once a month when they were at school together. Why hadn't she made her friends accept him like she had?

Maybe then he would have returned her texts and calls at university and maybe he would have contacted her about finding his brother. Maybe he would still be alive.

Maybe his death was all Bettie's fault.

"It isn't your fault auntie," Sean said as he hugged her.

Bettie kissed his hand as he walked around the opposite side of the kitchen island.

"Sometimes I think you know me too well," Bettie said.

"Maybe, Harry will be down in a minute,"

"How's he doing? And how are *you* doing?"

Sean shrugged. "His balance is back, everything he lost from the brain injury is back really. He was walking fine now. It's just his speech that is a little bad, but you already know all this. Why are you asking really?"

Bettie was almost offended but she knew it wasn't a bad question. "Honestly because I want a distraction from feeling like I should have done more for Frank over the years. And you know I love you and Harry like Elizabeth and Harrison,"

Sean smiled. "I love you too. Probably more than mum at times,"

Bettie half smiled at that. As much as she had issues with her sister Phryne for making Sean and harry live with them after the attack and brain injury, she honestly wouldn't change it for the world. It was as Phryne had said last August, she never wanted to become a mum so early and she wasn't even sure she was happy having a gay kid with an Italian boyfriend.

Bettie dismounted the bar stool and just hugged

Sean as she heard Graham stirring and then an idea popped into her head.

Graham, Harry and Zoey entered the kitchen and Bettie gestured everyone to come around the kitchen island and she pointed to the list of names.

"What if the reason why Frank never got to the other names on the list was because he found a DNA match?" Bettie asked.

"Actually I was too tired to notice earlier but now I'm sure there was a single missing hair sample when I was checking the results earlier," Zoey said.

"Good that means that this list contains the names of our suspects, our killers and most importantly the people who are going to be carrying out this attack," Bettie said.

Just saying that sent an icy cold shiver down Bettie's spine. They finally had their break in the case but they still didn't have Wi-Fi, phone service or anything they could use to track down these people or investigate them.

Graham took the notepad. "You know we could go down the police station and check out the paper records. If anyone had a criminal record or charge in the last two years it won't be too much work to find it. We might even be allowed to try out the backup generator and search a computer,"

Bettie looked at everyone else. That was their only chance and as much as she wanted Sean and Harry to come with them, she did need someone to look after the kids.

"Do you mind not coming?" Bettie asked, the guilt filling her voice.

"Actually I'll stay," Zoey said. "I'll watch the kids and it isn't like the man threatening me knows I went here,"

Bettie nodded. That was a good point.

Bettie quickly hugged her best friend, made sure her frying pan was close at hand and then they rushed out the already unlocked front door.

Bettie could have sworn she locked it earlier but she was in too much of a rush to think about it.

There was a crime to solve, people to save and a criminal to hunt down.

Exactly how Bettie liked it.

CHAPTER 11
00:30
18th February 2023

Canterbury, England

Graham was hardly impressed with his police friends as he led Bettie, Sean and Harry into the large box room that housed all of Kent Police's old criminal records that were uploaded onto the computer systems but hadn't been destroyed yet.

Even with their torches shining narrow strong, powerful beams into the darkness, Graham still couldn't believe how many rows upon rows of black metal shelves there were and they were going to have to sort through. And as much as he wanted to say that the elderly people that filed the records away were amazing and did everything, he knew that was a lie.

For all he knew there was nothing but jumbled-up records in each box regardless of the label on the front of it. This was going to be a long, chaotic night for sure.

It was even worse that because of budget cuts the police had gotten rid of the backup generator to help fund the purchase of three more drug dogs so they couldn't even check the computer systems. Graham hated all of this and he was going to make sure whoever attacked the power grid was going to pay.

"Everyone remember their names?" Bettie asked.

"Mine's Graham," Graham said.

Bettie playfully hit him.

"Fine, yes we remember the names you gave us to find," Graham said.

Everyone went off in different directions and Graham had to admit that this was just plain creepy. Walking about in the darkness just waiting to find the key to a murder case, none of this was good and Graham was just grateful none of them were virgins. This felt like a horror film in the making and virgins always died in horror films, or maybe it was the other way around.

Graham didn't know but he just wanted to find the names, find a key piece of evidence and get the hell out of here.

He went over to the A section that took up five whole shelves and he grabbed the first cardboard box and opened it.

The first name he needed to find was Alan Bennett. Graham had never heard the name before so hopefully they could eliminate him from their suspect pool.

"Why were there so many cops outside?" Sean

asked, his voice echoing in the darkness.

"Yeah," Bettie said from the other corner of the room. "I didn't know Canterbury had that many police officers,"

Graham just laughed because it was a fair point, it was rare for normal people to see just how many police officers there actually were these days. They were never on the street, never in public and most of the time people didn't know what cops looked like.

He knew he definitely hadn't known what a cop looked like until he was five and that was back in the 90s. Most kids these days didn't know what one looked like until they were much, much older.

"Found one name," Bettie said. "Dylan Fisher was arrested two years ago, released two months ago for assault,"

Graham kept looking through his own records. He couldn't see his first name but he did see another name that looked familiar.

He looked at the piece of paper with his names on them. He thought he recognised Collin Ashley, but he was actually looking for an Alan Ashley.

Graham couldn't find it and after half an hour of searching he couldn't find any of the names and no one else had shouted about finding their own names. So maybe Bettie had only found a single name out of the list.

"Is everyone done?" Graham asked.

"Yeah," everyone returned.

"Over here," Sean said.

Graham and the others went straight over to him and saw that Sean was sitting down on the ground with a few criminal records around him.

Everyone sat on the floor around him and Graham noticed that Frank had a criminal record himself. He took it and he was surprised that Frank had been arrested five years ago on suspicion of breaking into somewhere.

He passed it over to Bettie and she laughed. He had clearly missed something.

"Exactly," Sean said. "Frank was charged with breaking and entering into Protectus, someone calls the police and gets the charges dropped. Then he suddenly ends up working there a few years later,"

Graham nodded that was a good point and then he picked up some of the other criminal records and recognised some of these people.

Sean had pulled up all the well-known thieves in the area. Harry started tapping on a certain file and Graham took the file off him.

It was a file about a lawyer that wanted all of these people, including Frank, to be tried together and he had labelled them *The Destroyers*. Graham recognised the name, there had been a few online articles in Kent about how a group of young men were looking to attack the power grid so they could commit greater crimes.

The Destroyer wrote extensively about their manifesto, their ideas and more. They believed that electricity was being used incorrectly by society by protecting the rich instead of the poor and the people that needed the most protection.

Graham couldn't remember much more than that but judging by Bettie's beautifully concerned face she had come to the same conclusion.

"Do we think that Frank's brother is a member of the Destroyers and that's what got him killed?" Graham asked.

Bettie nodded. "I do. I think Frank was so obsessed with finding his brother that he just wanted to find him. No matter what he was involved in,"

"Trying save him," Harry said.

"Exactly babe," Sean said. "Maybe Frank was even trying to save his brother,"

"That is exactly the Frank I know," Bettie said.

"So how do we stop the Destroyers from doing another attack?" Sean asked.

Graham just smiled. He knew exactly where to start looking.

"Everything leads back to Protectus. We have to go there now," Graham said.

CHAPTER 12

00:45

18th February 2023

Canterbury, England

Toby Stevens just smiled to himself as he hid in a small little cupboard under Bettie English's stairs. It had been so easy to watch them, stare at Zoey's foul face and dream about her dying through Bettie's windows.

The watching had been the easiest part but all those dumb detectives and whoever the gay couple were all busy trying to solve whatever was going on, and whoever's life they were about to destroy for no good reason. Toby had simply picked the lock.

He was surprised it had been so easy considering Bettie English was meant to be some big hot shot private eye. It all just went to show that detectives are all as stupid as each other.

For the past few hours Toby had enjoyed the darkness of the small cupboard. There wasn't much in here so there was plenty of room for Toby to enjoy.

Through the little panels of door that allowed air to flow into the cupboard, he had watched Zoey try to get some sleep, she did some exercise in the darkness and she had even tried to do some cleaning.

She was such a wreck.

It was amazing that a woman like Zoey Quill could ever hope to achieve anything. It just approved how pathetic his father was that he had allowed himself to get caught by this excuse of a woman.

But sooner or later as the night went on and on Zoey Quill would continue to get tired, she would make a mistake and then Toby could kill her.

There was something about sleeping twins upstairs so he had to be quiet, as silent as the grave. He didn't want to wake them, he wanted the sweet little angels to sleep peacefully.

All whilst Zoey gasped and screamed out for air as Toby killed her.

That was going to be a very, very sweet moment indeed.

CHAPTER 13
02:00
18th February 2023
Canterbury, England

Bettie really wasn't pleased with the damn police station that refused to let them out back onto the streets because it was apparently too dangerous. Graham had had to promise they would be careful and they had a good reason for doing so.

After a long silly drive that was slowed down by three car crashes, two groups of middle-aged men threatening them with petrol bombs and a little old elderly woman preaching that this was the End Times. Bettie was finally standing outside the immense glass building that served as the Headquarters of Protectus.

The lights were off and looking at the building was like staring into a glass cube filled with black inky liquid. There was no light, no sign of life or sign of movement coming from inside. It was like the entire place was empty and always had been.

There was a single red car parked in the small car park that wasn't Graham's and the entire place felt a little weird.

"Here we go," Sean said as him and Harry finished hacking the lock that was shut down but there was barely enough power in the system to pop it open.

"There was a backup generator on earlier," Graham said.

"Why would Gloria turn it off?" Bettie asked.

Graham shrugged and Bettie really wished that she had a massive frying pan like Zoey. Instead she slipped her hand into her black purse and took out her pepper spray just in case.

All four of them went inside and Bettie was impressed with the white plastic tones and features of the lobby. It looked perfect and modern but a little too clinical for her liking.

Sean rushed over to the black fire door that Graham had mentioned earlier and it was locked shut.

"Gloria!" Bettie shouted.

Her voice echoed in the silence and she went over to Sean. "Can you force open the door?"

"That would be a crime," Sean said grinning.

"I think Gloria might be in danger so we're covered," Graham said.

Bettie doubted that but she wasn't going to argue. Sean slammed into the door a few times and Bettie wished she had bought her lockpicks but she had doubted she would need them.

"Button," Harry said pointing to a massive green button just left of the door.

Bettie pressed it and the door popped open with a hiss. She hugged Harry and they all went inside.

It was a massive server room of some kind with tall black computer towers running from the floor to ceiling with tons of different orange, white and blue flashing lights. At least there was some kind of backup power source in here.

There was a small central computer terminal in the middle of the room but it was Gloria's cold unconscious body behind it that concerned Bettie.

She went over to Gloria and checked for a pulse. Thankfully there was one but it was so faint and Bettie noticed there was a large pool of blood under her. Bettie carefully rolled her over and there was a tiny wound in Gloria's back.

"Could she have haemophilia?" Graham asked.

"It's possible but if that's true then maybe Frank didn't lose a brother at all," Bettie said.

Sean started tapping on the central computer terminal. "In fact she was checking out the same thing after Graham left. She was investigating the break-in that happened,"

"Wait," Bettie said. "So Gloria knew that Frank was the person that tried to break into Protectus five years ago and she still hired him,"

"Not uncommon. Computer hackers hired time," Harry said.

Bettie couldn't deny that it was common for hackers to get hired by different companies to improve their cybersecurity but again, Bettie just didn't believe Frank was a computer expert.

"Bring up Frank's personnel file," Bettie said.

"She was already looking at it because," Sean said pointing to the bottom of it, "it had his DNA on file for the biometrically sealed sections,"

Bettie just looked at the man she loved. "Graham, what exactly is Protectus?"

Everyone just stood in complete silence as it finally dawned on them that a small non-important computer place would never have biometrically sealed areas so only certain people could get access to them.

The lock on the door banged.

Bettie rushed over.

The fire door was locked.

Bettie saw something moving in the shadows.

They were locked in.

Locked in with no way to call for help. No one knew where they were. No emergency services could be called if they were found.

If they were ever found.

CHAPTER 14
02:15
18th February 2023

Canterbury, England

Leon Evans grinned as he walked out of the headquarters of Protectus. He couldn't believe that those dumb detectives had finally caught up with him. That was very strange, they were ahead of schedule.

Normally everyone else was too dumb compared to him so everyone was late according to his plans. But these people were early.

Of course Bettie English was nowhere near as smart, wonderful and brave as himself so there was no reason to worry. The plan would still be on track but he might just need to rearrange some things at the bank, the explosives and inform his mindless idiots that their most honoured guests might arrive a little sooner than expected.

But of course Bettie would probably think she was being so smart and clever that she was actually ahead of him. Leon just laughed at the very notion that a mere fool like Bettie could even begin to tell how smart he was.

He would get Bettie to the bank, he would trap her and then she would do his bidding like the little good girl he knew she could be given the right incense.

Everything else had fallen into place so perfectly. The blackout was perfect, the idiots of Canterbury were rioting and taking advantage of the situation and no one could call for help because of the phone service being down.

This was how society should be. This was how humanity was meant to live. None of these sissy laws controlling that most simple urge of man to attack, murder and commit wonderful crimes.

This was the life.

And Bettie English was not going to stop him. No matter what little Frank had said as Leon sliced his silly little head open.

He would succeed.

CHAPTER 15

02:15

18th February 2023

Canterbury, England

Graham slammed his fists into the damn fire door and he just couldn't believe that they were trapped for now. It was clear that someone was behind all of this and there had to be a connection, Graham just didn't know what the connection was.

Bettie stood up and Graham cocked his head at her.

"Sean," Bettie said. "Can you bring up Gloria's file?"

Sean did it and Graham noticed there was a top-secret folder that could only be accessed with her DNA. Sean clicked on the folder a small needle shot out of the computer terminal.

Bettie wiped some of Gloria's blood on it and Graham just hoped the DNA from Bettie's own skin cells wouldn't corrupt the reading too much.

It did. But it didn't matter.

"Bettie English DNA detected," the computer said in something close to Gloria's voice.

Graham was impressed.

All of them gathered around the computer terminal as a video of Gloria speaking appeared in this room.

"Bettie English you may be confused about what's going on but we needed you and only you in our task. Frank has always loved you deeply, he knew that if he or anyone he loved was in trouble then you were the only person to call,"

Graham placed a loving arm around her.

"Me and Frank set up this video failsafe when he discovered that this bother was part of the Protectus family and he was a founding member of the Destroyers,"

Graham gasped. They were finally getting a break in the case.

"Frank's brother goes by the name of Leon Evans, he worked for me ever since I founded the company and it was when Frank broke in once that he discovered Leon looked a lot like his father,"

Graham nodded. This was all starting to make perfect sense.

Gloria continued. "But by the time that Frank had returned a few years later, explained to me why he broke in in the first place and learnt that I too had a history with the security services. Leon was too embedded and powerful in the company to stop me too,"

Then Gloria paused and looked like she was about to say her darkest secret.

"And now Leon plans to commit the biggest crime in history to show that society is fragile, it can be destroyed and that the richest people can be made the poorest in a second," Gloria said.

Graham's hands formed fists.

"I did try to stop him but I failed and now we will kill him,"

The video stopped playing and Graham just hugged Bettie as she looked a little shaken.

"Leon was one of the names on the list," Sean said. "And it was ticked,"

Bettie pushed Graham away slightly. "This is a nightmare. So Frank found his brother, learnt he was a member of the Destroyers with their extreme ideology and presumably him trying to stop them got him killed,"

Graham nodded. It was the only thing that made sense.

"Bigger question is how would Leon show the world that society is fragile?" Graham asked.

Bettie shone her torch at Graham. "He already is. Look at just the drive over here. Without power it turns society into a madhouse. Car crashes, preaching old ladies, middle-aged groups threatening to kill you. Society is falling apart overnight,"

Graham shivered at the very idea of that. "But it still wouldn't explain how the rich become poor in a second?"

"Bank Destroy," Harry said.

"Oh shit," Graham said. "I read about the Kent Alliance Banking Firm redesigning their branch in Canterbury. The police keep some evidence stored there but so do billionaires and millionaires and moguls,"

"And a bank undergoing a redesign into a blackout would be a lot less secure that another bank in a blackout. He wants to attack a major bank," Bettie said.

"There has to be more than that," Sean said.

"Agreed but right now we have to get to the bank and stop them destroying it," Graham said.

Then everyone noticed that Harry was banging away on the computer and the fire door hissed opened and banged as it fell off the hinges.

Sean kissed Harry on the lips and all of them rushed out of there.

Graham just had to get to the bank no matter what happened next. He couldn't allow the robbery to happen.

And he just couldn't shake the feeling that something far worst was also happening here than a mere bank robbery.

CHAPTER 16
03:30
18th February 2023
Canterbury, England

Bettie had absolutely hated how long it had taken them to get from the outskirts of Canterbury to the high street all because of some dumb new police barricade they had set up to protect the shops.

It had taken ages to convince the stupid cops on duty that they weren't thieves but thankfully Kinsley had noticed and waved them all through. Even Graham's police radio hadn't worked at convincing the cops what had happened, several of them had been stolen through the night.

A little fact that worried Bettie a lot more than she ever wanted to admit.

"Here it is," Sean said as they all marched up the high street passing tons of little ancient shops in their dark reds, whites and blues.

Bettie folded her arms as she looked at the

impressively gothic bank just off of the high street but so close to it that it basically was on the high street.

The bank had immense concrete dragons lining the outside of it, scaffolding cladded the rest of the normally white marble outside in thick canvas sheets and metal making it look ugly.

Bettie didn't even see a doorway. The only entrance into the bank might have laid beyond the small metal railings and fencing that stopped someone from getting to close.

But Bettie couldn't understand why there was a large white van parked further down the road.

Bettie pointed to the van and Graham, Sean and Harry nodded. They had travelled all over Canterbury tonight and from everything they had seen a white van just looked so out of place.

The four of them slowly went over to it. Bettie's heart started to beat faster and faster in her chest and she really hoped it was connected to the case.

She could handle a criminal, a dead body or even weapons. Yet she didn't want it to be empty. If it was empty then she was just concerned about where everything inside and everyone had gone to.

Bettie looked at the others as she reached for the black door handle at the back, she got out her pepper spray and prepared to strike.

She opened it.

It was completely empty except for a small little red present wrapped up with a perfect tiny bow. There was no note, no signature, no sign of what was inside.

"That's just damn creepy," Graham said.

Bettie could only agree as she gestured she was going to open it. She wanted to open it, she really did but she couldn't help but feel like this was a trap.

"Be on the lookout for anyone," Bettie said.

The others only nodded and their hands formed fists as if that was actually going to put people off of attacking.

Bettie touched the silky soft wrapping paper, undid the carefully tied bow and she popped up the present. To reveal it was empty and there was nothing inside at all.

But then she realised that Harry, Sean and Graham were all looking at her instead of keeping their eyes peeled on the surrounding areas. That was exactly what Leon wanted.

He was clever, too damn clever and now Bettie just knew that something bad was going to happen.

She spun around.

And saw five men dressed in all black were halfway down the road coming towards them.

Bettie and the others started running in the opposite direction but ten other men were walking up.

They were trapped and they all had guns. Then they stopped.

"Bettie English," a man said from above but Bettie couldn't see him. "My brother really loved you, treasured you, worshipped you. And that was why he had to die he was convinced that you would save him and me so I had to kill him to stop that,"

Bettie frowned. Leon Evans was a madman that was for sure.

"I trust you will come silently with me and my men," the voice said.

Bettie looked at Graham and the two men that were basically her own children and she nodded at them. everything would be okay and he was still a haemophilic at the end of the day.

She only needed to cut him and hopefully save them all.

"Bring them inside. If they struggle kill them all except Bettie," Leon said.

Bettie just wanted to end this solve now but she had to learn exactly what Frank had died to bring to her attention.

She owned him that much at the very least.

CHAPTER 17
03:45
18th February 2023
Canterbury, England

Graham was amazed at the sheer grandeur of the bright white and golden marble that shone like diamonds in the torchlight as Leon's foul men pushed him, Bettie, Sean and Harry into the reception area of the bank where everything seemed to glow.

There were random pieces of white canvas sheet flapping in the cold nightly breeze and Graham really wasn't a fan of the dusty smell in the air that couldn't be safe to breathe but he made himself forget about that little scary fact.

Leon's men forced them all to stop in the centre of the reception area and Graham just stared at all the horrible men in their black gear. The guns weren't too much of a problem because they were only Glocks, not automatic rifles but he still had to protect the woman and family he loved.

"This is a problem you know," a male voice said.

Graham looked in the direction of the voice and was stunned to see Leon Evans in the flesh. The madman that had murdered his own brother, bought down a substation and destroyed mobile phone coverage in Canterbury.

Graham was surprised that Leon was relatively short wearing black military boots, black jeans and a black shirt that would make him one with the night if it wasn't for the torchlight.

Leon gave Graham an evil grin. "You and your nephew are very, very expendable here so don't try here anything,"

"Why?" Bettie asked. "Why do all of this?"

Graham looked around the bank as Leon carefully considered his answer. And he noticed that he had actually seen the plans to this bank before in police paperwork, there was a steel staircase that led directly down in the police storage area.

The only reason why police evidence was being stored here during the redesign because was the police vault wasn't touched at all and it would be sealed up tighter than Fort Knox.

"The police vault," Graham said. "You intend to get into that. Why? Who do you want to free?"

Leon laughed. "We all have our friends and true family. Not that silly blood family that everyone is obsessed with. I have my true family behind bars,"

Graham nodded. This wasn't a bank heist or about furthering the Destroyer's agenda. This was all about accessing evidence to an upcoming trial involving this extremist group.

"You can't get access to the police vault," Graham said.

Leon laughed hard. "Of course I can't. It was one of the reasons why I killed Frank because his death could bring you to me,"

"Fuck," Graham said finally realising that Leon had relied on them being too good.

"It's even better because I thought you two would arrive at 6 am not now," Leon said clapping his hands together.

Graham looked at Sean and Harry who were in tight headlocks and a gun pressed into their mouths.

"Right then," Leon said, "the task is simple you two have 30 minutes to get into the police vault or I kill Sean and Harry. Then you Graham have another 30 minutes before I kill Bettie,"

"Bastard," Graham said.

"A lot of people have called me that," Leon said.

Then two firm hands gripped Graham's shoulders and started pulling him and Bettie towards the steel staircase that led straight down into the police vault.

Graham knew exactly how impossible this was going to be. Kent Police had picked this place because it was so damn secure and it had three levels of security.

Each harder than the last one.

When Graham was stopped in front of a massive

steel door designed to look like elevator doors he simply took out his police ID and placed his right hand on the door.

He felt the icy coldness of the door scan his hand and double check that his police ID was real and then it opened.

Revealed a very narrow and long staircase down to the depths of the police vaults.

"There are still two more security levels to clear," Graham said.

Leon nodded as five of his men joined him, Graham and Bettie walked down the staircase.

"Also Graham if you try anything I will kill Bettie in front of you," Leon said.

Graham just smiled to himself because Leon clearly had no idea who the hell he was messing with.

He just hoped that he could buy himself enough time to come up with a plan to save them all. And not get the woman and family he loved killed in the process.

A massive ask.

CHAPTER 18
04:00

18th February 2023

Canterbury, England

"15 minutes until your family dies," Leon said.

Bettie was seriously starting to get annoyed at Leon now. He was just a massive idiot that she was so looking forward to seeing behind bars but they had to survive this first.

Graham had led them all down the very narrow and rusty (fake) steel staircase that led them down onto a small circular metal platform with a small computer terminal on it.

Bettie loved security measures as much as the next girl but this was a nightmare with Sean and Harry's life in danger. At least those two boys weren't stupid, they were clever, smart and had some self-defence training after last year's attack. Bettie just wanted them to be okay more than ever. She really did love them like her own children.

As Graham started typing with three whole fingers on the computer terminal (Bettie hated how he typed) she focused on the black sooty circular walls of the staircase. They were ugly and none of this felt right.

"Don't get fooled little lady," one of Leon's men said. "These walls are deadly and if you're naughty for daddy I'll pin you up against one as the electricity flooded your body,"

Bettie so badly wanted to punch him.

A bullet went off.

The man's corpse smashed onto the ground.

Leon put his gun away and weakly grinned at Bettie. "You're welcome,"

Bettie nodded her thanks. She was more concerned about how mad Leon really was, if he was so willing to kill someone working for him. Would he even think about killing her, Graham and the boys?

She doubted it.

"I need the case number," Graham said.

Leon marched over to Graham and pushed him out the way. He started typing away but he laughed when the computer didn't respond to him.

"It only responds to a cop's DNA," Bettie said.

Leon shook his head and just emptied his gun into the computer terminal and as sparks lit up the staircase from the destruction out of the small backup generator powering the terminal. Bettie just shook her head.

Leon was just flat out dangerous.

A few moments later the entire staircase vibrated as a small door opened in the platform that made the stairs turn into a long spiral staircase.

"Get moving," Leon said.

Bettie went first and as she went further and further down into the darkness of the stairs she couldn't imagine what Leon was really after.

But the massive metre-wide gap in the middle of the spiral staircase made Bettie uneasy. It was perfect pushing someone down there but the staircase looked so tall that a drop from this height would probably kill them.

Leon seemed to be way way too smart and unstable to actually want to free someone because he didn't seem to care about someone. He killed his brother. He killed his worker. He was going to kill innocent people.

Bettie just couldn't understand why Leon would do all of this to free someone. Unless he wasn't. And with less than 15 minutes to get into the police vault to save Sean's and Harry's life Bettie really wasn't liking the odds of her figuring this out in time.

But then she realised she had all the power here.

Bettie stopped on the spiral staircase and just looked at Leon as everyone focused their torches on her and Graham.

"Come on Graham we're going back up," Bettie said like she was deadly serious.

This probably wasn't the best plan but she wanted to try something.

Leon took out his gun and pointed it at Graham's head. "You aren't,"

"Yeah we are," Bettie said. "Your men would have to literally drag us down these stairs,"

Leon nodded. "Fine then. Drag her down,"

Bettie subtly went closer to Graham. "Just remember to push,"

Graham nodded like he understood what she was planning.

As three of the big strapping men in their black gear pushed past Bettie and Graham Leon just watched them like they were all pieces of meat to be killed.

As soon as a man was right in front of Bettie she charged forward.

Jumping forward.

Graham did the same twice.

The men lost their balance.

They fell backwards.

They fell against the metal railing Bettie hadn't noticed.

It snapped.

The men screamed.

Their bones crunched as they smashed into the ground below.

Leon laughed as he reloaded his gun and shot the last remaining man that was loyal to him.

"That was very very good you know," Leon said. "At least I don't have to pay them now and thank you,"

Bettie's skin went icy cold as the realisation that they were now alone with a madman with a gun sank in. A gun he was very happy to use.

CHAPTER 19
04:05
18th February 2023
Canterbury, England

Zoey Quill felt so damn tired as she laid on Bettie's wonderfully large black sofa. She hadn't managed to get much sleep at all tonight and as she laid there noticing how all the tealights, candles and sweet vanilla scent that filled the air, she couldn't help but think that she had overreacted to the death threats.

It was clear that no one had broken into Bettie's house, no one was coming for her and she was perfectly safe here.

Zoey just allowed the full sofa to take all her weight. It was so nice just to relax after a day like today after all the tests she had to run at work, the blackout and stress that caused and how badly she just wanted to go home and be with her husband and kids.

Actually that wasn't a bad idea really. No one was coming for her after all so she would be perfectly okay.

Zoey still had her car on the driveway and if she wrote a quick note then Bettie would know that she wasn't kidnapped or dead. She had simply gone home to be with her loved ones.

She stood up and she really missed the softness of the sofa but she just had to go home. There was no point carrying the frying pan into the kitchen to write out the note because she was perfectly safe.

Zoey went into the kitchen, grabbed one of Frank's notepads and sat on a barstool at the wonderful kitchen island.

She started writing the note when she could have sworn she had seen something out of the corner of her eye. She looked around but there was nothing there. Yet she didn't like it at all that one by one the candles were slowly dying out.

Someone tackled her to the ground.

Knocking the bar stool out from under her.

Zoey smashed onto the ground.

Her wrist protested in pain.

Pain flooded her body.

Two massive hands gripped her throat.

Smashing her head into the floor.

Again and again.

Zoey kicked. Struggled.

Screamed.

No sound was coming out.

The grip tightened around her throat.

Zoey slashed the attacker's face with her nails.

He screamed.

Zoey kept slashing wildly.

Blood splattered over her face.

She whacked the man's elbows.

He fell forward.

Releasing her throat.

Zoey threw him off her.

She leapt up.

Charging into the living room.

The man tackled her.

There was no light in the living room. She couldn't see the frying pan.

The man climbed on her back.

Grabbing her face.

Zoey felt around for the frying pan.

She felt something cold at the edge of her fingers.

The man tensed.

She was going to die. Her heart thundered in her chest.

She couldn't die. She loved her kids. She had to see them grow up.

The man laughed.

He was enjoying this. He was going to kill her.

Zoey had to act. She had to save herself.

She wasn't going to make her husband a widow.

Zoey threw her weight forward.

She grabbed something cold.

She swung it.

The man screamed.

Something crunched behind her.

The man fell off her.

Zoey leapt up.

Climbed on top of him.

She smashed down the frying pan again and again.

Until it was no longer hitting face.

She was hitting a very wet floor.

CHAPTER 20

04:15

18th February 2023

Canterbury, England

"Time's up," Leon said.

Bettie just wanted to punch this guy so damn badly as the three of them reached the end of the spiral staircase leading down to the police vault. And Bettie just stared with surprise at the immense steel vault door that was easily three times the height of her.

This was going to be impossible to crack and open and surely they were all doomed.

Bettie just looked at Leon as he stepped off the final step and he smiled like this was his crowning achievement even though he still wasn't inside.

And Bettie had no intention of letting him get inside.

"Open it then," Leon said.

Graham shrugged and just leant against the vault

door. Bettie did the same, hissing as the sheer coldness of the metal surprised her.

"You cannot open it, I'm guessing," Bettie said.

Graham nodded. "It took me a while to remember how police evidence lockups work. It's been a long time since I got anything out of one. But you cannot open this one,"

Leon frowned and pointed it at Graham's head. Bettie smiled. Leon was finally starting to let emotion cloud his judgement and if he could focus on Graham just a little longer then Bettie could jump him or something.

"You can't open it because you didn't enter the case number on the computer terminal. You must know how bureaucratic police systems are. No number, no access," Graham said.

Leon's frown deepened. "Get it open!"

Graham shook his head and was brave enough to take a step forward.

Bettie did too so she was within striking distance.

"We tried to help you," Bettie said. "But you weren't smart enough to realise that you needed to not destroy stuff,"

Leon laughed. "I am smart. I am the smartest person alive. I will figure out a way inside the vault,"

"Why?" Bettie asked really curious now.

"Because I will burn this evidence. Then the criminals locked away will demand a retrial and because the evidence is destroyed they will walk free. Then and only then will anarchy return to *man*kind,"

Bettie just shook her head. This sad little deluded man was a crazy one at that. He really did believe he was so smart that he could bring about the downfall of society with a simple bank robbery.

It was stupid but Bettie understood it.

If they allowed him into the police vault then so many sex offenders, murderers and other foul abominations could go free.

"You cannot-" Bettie said.

"Yes I can! Yes I can! I can do whatever I want you little dumb bitch,"

Graham charged forward.

Tackling Leon to the ground.

Bettie grabbed the gun and pointed it firmly at Leon.

"Get off me! Get off me!" Leon shouted.

Then the entire bank hummed, banged and vibrated as the lights turned back on and Leon looked so defeated like everything he had ever wanted to achieve had failed.

Because that was exactly what had happened.

"Did we ever tell you that Sean and Harry are some of the most resourceful men I know?" Bettie said.

"And did your research into us tell you that Sean and Harry are some of the best students their university has ever had," Graham said.

"And did my auntie and Graham tell you that it wasn't hard to figure out how to reactivate the substation," Sean said as him and Harry walked down the staircase with Detective Kinsley right behind them.

Bettie was so damn happy that Sean and Harry were okay.

Leon shook his head. "No. This cannot be happening. I threw a shopping trolley into the substation, things exploded and I faked a cyberattack affecting the few computer systems in the substation,"

"That's exactly what we realised after a while," Sean said hugging Harry. "And the reaction of your men confirmed that theory, so after Kinsley and the police stormed in. I contacted the substation using Kinsley's sat-phone and told them to forget about the cyberattack and just focus on replacing the damaged and exploded parts,"

"Already doing that," Harry said.

Leon just frowned like a little child had been stopped from playing by its parents.

"It's not fair," Leon said.

Bettie laughed and just gestured Kinsley should take him away and finally Leon could be put away in prison exactly where he belonged for a very, very long time.

CHAPTER 21
05:00
18th February 2023

Canterbury, England

As Graham leant against the cold brick wall of a closed shop on the high street with his arms wrapped round wonderful Bettie, that he loved more than anything else in the entire world, and Sean and Harry were hugging next to them too. He just focused on the five surviving bad guys and Leon being taken away and the five corpses leaving in body bags.

There was no one else on the cobblestone high street beside of them and police officers. Graham definitely wasn't a fan of the creepy silence that was only punctuated by Bettie's relaxing breathing.

Yet Graham had to admit that the silence was exactly what he needed after the chaos of the past few hours, giving statements and telling the police exactly what had happened and how they had saved the day.

He even wondered if a lot of people in

Canterbury would realise just how long the blackout lasted. He really hoped not a lot of people.

It was still dark but bright pink streaks in the distance threatened to veil the sky in light later on so Graham was excited about that. He was so done with the darkness, and he just wanted to walk about without needing a torch or something.

Thankfully the bright white streetlights were working again and his eyes were hurting slightly. He hadn't realised how much he had been straining his eyes over the past twelve hours because of the blackout.

He felt so tired that he honestly doubted he could even drive them all back safely, but he was going to try. And he had heard something about someone being killed at Bettie's house but because only a corner had been called and not a crime scene unit he knew that Zoey was thankfully okay physically.

He just hoped that she wasn't too shaken up by whatever had happened.

Graham just hugged Bettie tighter as he realised just how weird the entire case had been. It had all started with Frank just wanting to find his brother again and he had found him, a strange crazy madman that was a foul sexist pig that wanted to return the world to a state of lawlessness.

He was so thick and dumb.

Graham knew from what everything Bettie had told him that Frank was a good man so he probably wanted to save his brother. He stuck around hoping to convince Leon that what he was doing was wrong and he must have mentioned Bettie once or twice.

Graham didn't blame Frank in the slightest at all. He had just tried to do the right thing and his brother had killed him for it and then set up a series of events to make sure him and Bettie went to the bank in the end.

Leon was clearly smart in some small way. It was just a massive shame that he didn't put that intelligence to good use.

"I found out why Frank broke into Protectus all those years ago," Bettie said quietly as Graham kissed her neck.

"Why?" Graham asked realising just how tired he was.

"Because it was a test. The firm had top-secret government contracts, hence the biometrically secured areas so they needed Frank to test the system. It worked well but improvements did need to be made,"

Graham nodded. That explanation was probably the simplest thing about this case.

A small beep of police sirens filled the air as the police van, armed response and the corpse van (as Graham called it) drove away and then another police car drove up with Kinsley inside.

"Fancy a lift?" Kinsley asked.

Graham nodded and all four of them jumped inside. He would get his car later on but right now, he just wanted a little nap and he knew the move his head hit that headrest him and Bettie were so going to fall asleep.

For just a moment Graham almost felt bad for Kinsley having to drive them back to their place with no one to talk to. But judging by how well Kinsley, Harry and Sean were getting on he really doubted that was a problem and it was wonderful. It was a wonderful sign that everything was back to normal, exactly how it should be.

CHAPTER 22
06:30
18 February 2023
Canterbury, England

Bettie had never ever realised until now exactly how beautiful her copper-finished kitchen was before. It looked so amazingly perfect with the early morning light after a great nap and Bettie felt like a brand-new woman after a little nap.

She definitely knew that she would be having a few more naps throughout the day as she tried to recover from the excitement, but she was so looking forward to those naps. They were honestly going to be the best naps of her little life.

Graham sat across from her and even with the beautiful copper cabinets and cupboards reflecting the morning light so perfectly, he was still the most beautiful, perfect and lovely thing in the entire world.

He was so beautiful, especially as he had made

her a nice cup of coffee as soon as they got home. He really was a darling like that. And was a darling about a lot of things, that was exactly why Bettie knew she was going to marry him at some point.

She was more than happy that Harry and Sean were upstairs sleeping, they deserved to sleep all day after what they had achieved whilst being taken hostage. They were amazing and she loved them both so damn much.

Kinsley had gone home and him and Sean and Harry had all given each other a mischievous smile as he left. Bettie wasn't sure she wanted to know the details of the conversation they had had in the car when her and Graham were asleep but it was clearly adult. And Bettie didn't have a problem with it at all, everyone deserved to have a little fun at times.

The morning was even better when Bettie had had a call from the hospital saying that Gloria had been found thanks to her tip off, she had been treated and she was going to make a full recovery. And she was only too eager to testify against Leon including how he had told her about installing software on Frank's computer.

Bettie imagined that she would but it was great that Gloria hadn't died. This case already had a high body count, anything above zero was too high for Bettie's liking.

She took a sip of her delicious bitter coffee and she heard someone stirred some upstairs she was pleased that Zoey seemed to be okay after killing her attacker. Bettie was definitely going to press her to talk about it because killing someone always changed a person.

Bettie was never going to allow her best friend to suffer in silence, and if Zoey needed it then she would hook up Zoey with one of the Federation's top psychologists. It was just something Bettie did for her friends.

"I'm still amazed that the crime scene clean-up crews got here so fast," Graham said.

Bettie nodded. She was surprised that the living room looked as good as new and it was one less room that needed cleaning later on.

"I think it's more of a thank you from the police commissioner for solving this," Graham said.

Bettie could only nod to that. She didn't care why it had happened, she was just grateful that it had.

Bettie stood up and went over to the man she loved and she kissed his sexy lips. "You know what I'm really pleased with,"

"What?" Graham asked smiling.

"That the twins have slept through the entire thing and we didn't have to settle them once," Bettie said.

Graham laughed. "True but you know they're oversleeping,"

Bettie gasped and shook her head as she realised that she was still tired, her precious little babies were about to wake up full of life and energy and passion, and she still had a lot of sleeping to catch up on.

"God I love being a parent," Bettie said, meaning every single word of it.

"Me too," Graham said kissing her as the sound of babies babbling loudly shook through the entire house.

Bettie's little precious angels were awake and she was so glad that everything was back to normal. The power was back on, the phone service was restored and the criminals were locked up forever. Life really didn't get any better than that and Bettie loved the wonderful feeling it gave her.

GET YOUR FREE SHORT STORY NOW! And get signed up to Connor Whiteley's newsletter to hear about new gripping books, offers and exciting projects. (You'll never be sent spam)

https://www.subscribepage.com/wintersignup

About the author:

Connor Whiteley is the author of over 60 books in the sci-fi fantasy, nonfiction psychology and books for writer's genre and he is a Human Branding Speaker and Consultant.

He is a passionate warhammer 40,000 reader, psychology student and author.

Who narrates his own audiobooks and he hosts The Psychology World Podcast.

All whilst studying Psychology at the University of Kent, England.

Also, he was a former Explorer Scout where he gave a speech to the Maltese President in August 2018 and he attended Prince Charles' 70th Birthday Party at Buckingham Palace in May 2018.

Plus, he is a self-confessed coffee lover!

<u>Other books by Connor Whiteley:</u>
<u>Bettie English Private Eye Series</u>
A Very Private Woman
The Russian Case
A Very Urgent Matter
A Case Most Personal
Trains, Scots and Private Eyes
The Federation Protects
Cops, Robbers and Private Eyes
Just Ask Bettie English
An Inheritance To Die For
The Death of Graham Adams
Bearing Witness
The Twelve
The Wrong Body
The Assassination Of Bettie English

<u>Lord of War Origin Trilogy:</u>
Not Scared Of The Dark
Madness
Burn Them All

<u>The Fireheart Fantasy Series</u>
Heart of Fire
Heart of Lies
Heart of Prophecy
Heart of Bones
Heart of Fate

<u>City of Assassins (Urban Fantasy)</u>

City of Death
City of Marytrs
City of Pleasure
City of Power

Agents of The Emperor
Return of The Ancient Ones
Vigilance
Angels of Fire
Kingmaker
The Eight
The Lost Generation
Hunt
Emperor's Council
Speaker of Treachery
Birth Of The Empire
Terraforma

The Rising Augusta Fantasy Adventure Series
Rise To Power
Rising Walls
Rising Force
Rising Realm

Lord Of War Trilogy (Agents of The Emperor)

Not Scared Of The Dark
Madness
Burn It All Down

Gay Romance Novellas
Breaking, Nursing, Repairing A Broken Heart
Jacob And Daniel
Fallen For A Lie
Spying And Weddings

The Garro Series- Fantasy/Sci-fi
GARRO: GALAXY'S END
GARRO: RISE OF THE ORDER
GARRO: END TIMES
GARRO: SHORT STORIES
GARRO: COLLECTION
GARRO: HERESY
GARRO: FAITHLESS
GARRO: DESTROYER OF WORLDS
GARRO: COLLECTIONS BOOK 4-6
GARRO: MISTRESS OF BLOOD
GARRO: BEACON OF HOPE
GARRO: END OF DAYS

Winter Series- Fantasy Trilogy Books
WINTER'S COMING
WINTER'S HUNT
WINTER'S REVENGE
WINTER'S DISSENSION

Miscellaneous:
RETURN
FREEDOM
SALVATION
Reflection of Mount Flame
The Masked One
The Great Deer
English Independence

OTHER SHORT STORIES BY CONNOR WHITELEY

Mystery Short Story Collections
Criminally Good Stories Volume 1: 20 Detective Mystery Short Stories
Criminally Good Stories Volume 2: 20 Private Investigator Short Stories
Criminally Good Stories Volume 3: 20 Crime Fiction Short Stories
Criminally Good Stories Volume 4: 20 Science Fiction and Fantasy Mystery Short Stories
Criminally Good Stories Volume 5: 20 Romantic Suspense Short Stories

Mystery Short Stories:
Protecting The Woman She Hated
Finding A Royal Friend
Our Woman In Paris
Corrupt Driving
A Prime Assassination

Jubilee Thief
Jubilee, Terror, Celebrations
Negative Jubilation
Ghostly Jubilation
Killing For Womenkind
A Snowy Death
Miracle Of Death
A Spy In Rome
The 12:30 To St Pancreas
A Country In Trouble
A Smokey Way To Go
A Spicy Way To GO
A Marketing Way To Go
A Missing Way To Go
A Showering Way To Go
Kendra Detective Mystery Collection Volume 1
Kendra Detective Mystery Collection Volume 2
Stealing A Chance At Freedom
Glassblowing and Death
Theft of Independence
Cookie Thief
Marble Thief
Book Thief
Art Thief
Mated At The Morgue
The Big Five Whoopee Moments
Stealing An Election
Mystery Short Story Collection Volume 1
Mystery Short Story Collection Volume 2
Criminal Performance

Candy Detectives
Key To Birth In The Past

Science Fiction Short Stories:
Temptation
Superhuman Autospy
Blood In The Redwater
All Is Dust
Vigil
Emperor Forgive Us
Their Brave New World
Gummy Bear Detective
The Candy Detective
What Candies Fear
The Blurred Image
Shattered Legions
The First Rememberer
Life of A Rememberer
System of Wonder
Lifesaver
Remarkable Way She Died
The Interrogation of Annabella Stormic
Blade of The Emperor
Arbiter's Truth
Computation of Battle
Old One's Wrath
Puppets and Masters
Ship of Plague
Interrogation
Fantasy Short Stories:

City of Snow

City of Light

City of Vengeance

Dragons, Goats and Kingdom

Smog The Pathetic Dragon

Don't Go In The Shed

The Tomato Saver

The Remarkable Way She Died

The Bloodied Rose

Asmodia's Wrath

Heart of A Killer

Emissary of Blood

Dragon Coins

Dragon Tea

Dragon Rider

Sacrifice of the Soul

Heart of The Flesheater

Heart of The Regent

Heart of The Standing

Feline of The Lost

Heart of The Story

City of Fire

Awaiting Death

All books in 'An Introductory Series':

Careers In Psychology
Psychology of Suicide
Dementia Psychology
Clinical Psychology Reflections Volume 4
Forensic Psychology of Terrorism And Hostage-Taking
Forensic Psychology of False Allegations
Year In Psychology
CBT For Anxiety
CBT For Depression
Applied Psychology
BIOLOGICAL PSYCHOLOGY 3RD EDITION
COGNITIVE PSYCHOLOGY THIRD EDITION
SOCIAL PSYCHOLOGY- 3RD EDITION
ABNORMAL PSYCHOLOGY 3RD EDITION
PSYCHOLOGY OF RELATIONSHIPS- 3RD EDITION
DEVELOPMENTAL PSYCHOLOGY 3RD EDITION
HEALTH PSYCHOLOGY
RESEARCH IN PSYCHOLOGY
A GUIDE TO MENTAL HEALTH AND TREATMENT AROUND THE WORLD- A GLOBAL LOOK AT DEPRESSION
FORENSIC PSYCHOLOGY
THE FORENSIC PSYCHOLOGY OF THEFT, BURGLARY AND OTHER CRIMES AGAINST PROPERTY
CRIMINAL PROFILING: A FORENSIC PSYCHOLOGY GUIDE TO FBI PROFILING

AND GEOGRAPHICAL AND STATISTICAL
PROFILING.
CLINICAL PSYCHOLOGY
FORMULATION IN PSYCHOTHERAPY
PERSONALITY PSYCHOLOGY AND
INDIVIDUAL DIFFERENCES
CLINICAL PSYCHOLOGY REFLECTIONS
VOLUME 1
CLINICAL PSYCHOLOGY REFLECTIONS
VOLUME 2
Clinical Psychology Reflections Volume 3
CULT PSYCHOLOGY
Police Psychology

A Psychology Student's Guide To University
How Does University Work?
A Student's Guide To University And Learning
University Mental Health and Mindset

Milton Keynes UK
Ingram Content Group UK Ltd.
UKHW010502080224
437425UK00016B/438

9 781916 847019